TRUPP

A FUZZHEAD TALE

WRITTEN AND ILLUSTRATED BY

JANELL CANNON

SCHOLASTIC INC.

New York · Toronto · London · Auckland · Sydney

ISBN 0-590-89934-1

12 11 10 9 8 7 6 5 4 3 2 1   6 7 8 9/9 0 1/0

Printed in the U.S.A.   08

First Scholastic printing, October 1996

TO
Pat and Jim Hansen

FOR SANCTUARY

Fuzzhead

(Blancofelis dexterodactylus)
Average adult weight: 200 lbs. • *Average adult height:* 6' (standing)

These catlike creatures have a dense coat of soft, white fur and crystalline blue eyes. Their front feet (or hands) have opposable thumbs, which allow dexterous handling of tools. Although omnivorous, they subsist primarily on fruits and vegetables.

The Fuzzhead population is estimated to be quite small. Counts are not accurate because of the inaccessibility of these highly secretive beings whose life span is rumored to be as long as two hundred years. Nonconfrontational and peace-loving, they have lived in harmony through the millennia with animals humans consider wild.

Highly adaptable to a wide range of climatic and geographic conditions, Fuzzheads live on every continent of the world. They are exceptionally intelligent and possess highly developed language skills. Although their language is globally uniform and largely unpronounceable to humans, Fuzzheads learn all languages with ease. The name Fuzzhead is of human origin. It was adopted by humans because of their difficulty understanding the creature's own name for itself.

It all started when Trupp began to wonder
how big the world was. Gazing out over the red
cliffs of his home, Trupp tried and tried to imagine what
might be beyond. His head hurt from thinking so hard.
Finally he decided to see for himself.

Trupp marched to the Family Cave, where he found Eep, Urt, Rau, Trau, and Mau. Little Yau slipped in just in time to hear Trupp announce, "I want to go past the red cliffs."

The Old Ones looked at one another. Then Trau told Trupp, "You have learned to survive on your own, but you know little about humans. Most people who see us fear us."

Urt explained, "If you wear clothes, however, they will not see who you are. They won't even notice you."

"Their pets may recognize you anyway," warned Mau. "You must be very careful."

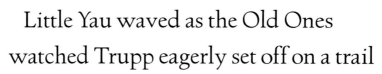

Little Yau waved as the Old Ones
watched Trupp eagerly set off on a trail
that led away from the Family Cave.
He scrambled up the red rock cliffs and
teetered along the narrow canyon ledge.
His strong claws kept him from falling.

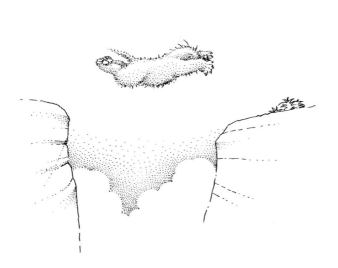

When the land became flatter and greener,
Trupp found cool, grassy places to rest at night.
He was enchanted by cricket songs in the
moonlight.

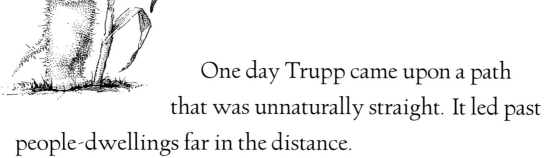

One day Trupp came upon a path
that was unnaturally straight. It led past
people-dwellings far in the distance.

"Uh-oh," Trupp said. "Time to find some clothes."

He started down the path in search of a disguise.

Soon Trupp found something very strange standing near tall rows of corn. A large, black bird was perched by its head.

"Don't be scared," called the bird. "This old scarecrow doesn't scare me, 'cause I'm a raven. Ever hear of a scareraven? *Krawk-awk-awk-awk!*" He laughed.

"No," Trupp answered, "but I must find some clothes to wear so people won't be afraid of me."

"Well then, use these," the bird replied, pointing his wing at the scarecrow.

With the raven's help Trupp struggled into the pants and shirt. He covered his fuzzy white head with the hat.

The bird flew away and returned carrying a towel. He wrapped it around the scarecrow and said, "Don't want him to catch a chill." He lit on Trupp's shoulder. "And by the way, I come with the clothes. Call me Krok."

"How do you do, Krok? I'm pleased to have you as a companion," Trupp replied as he headed for the unnaturally straight path.

Large boxes on wheels now stood on the path. The raven fluttered aboard one that had an open door.

"All aboard!" said Krok. "This train will take us fast and far."

As Trupp stretched to climb up, the pants ripped. A cool breeze tickled his tail.

Slowly the big boxcar began to move with a sound like thunder. As the train picked up speed, the green land went by in a blur.

After a long time the train came to a halt with great screeching and crashing. They were in a gray, quiet place.

When Trupp leaped to the ground, he howled in pain. A clear, sharp stone had stuck in his foot.

"Broken glass," mumbled Krok. "You have to watch out for that stuff here."

"*Ow-wow-wow,*" Trupp cried as he picked the sliver out with his claws.

In no time Trupp and Krok found busy streets crowded with people. The humans rushed past, their shoes clopping on the concrete.

Trupp was amazed that they all thought he was one of them.

"They don't even notice *me*," cackled Krok.

Thirsty and covered with dust, Trupp and Krok were
delighted to find a pool of water. They drank and took a bath.
"Can't you read the sign?" shouted an angry voice.
"No swimming in the fountain!" A man in
stiff blue clothes and shiny black shoes
stood glaring at Trupp. "Kids these days!
Don't even know how to read! I'll just have
to notify the authorities," the man growled as
he stomped away.
"He must be hot, too," said Trupp.

Not far from the fountain a woman in a red hat and a tiny dog with a red bow on its head sat on a bench. The woman was throwing bread on the grass.

"What a generous person," Trupp said to Krok as they hungrily snapped up a few pieces.

But the woman yelled, "Hey, kid! Get outta here! You shouldn't be eating food off the ground. And tell your mama to fix your pants."

The little dog snarled, "*Ah-rugga-rugga-rugga! Ah-rarf-rarf-rarf!*"

"He sees me," gasped Trupp. "We'd better run."

Trupp and Krok fled back into the streets.

But a big woman blocked their path. "Well, well, well," she said. "I see your kind in town every once in a while. You're one of those cat-things."

Trupp froze. This person saw who he really was.

Looking around for an escape, Trupp noticed the ground glittered with broken glass. The people-dwellings were splashed everywhere with brilliant colors. Dark shadows stretched between the tall buildings.

Trupp couldn't decide whether to stay or run away.

"My name is Bernice," said the woman. "If you go running off, your feet will get even more cut up than they already are. Let me see your paw."

Bernice seemed to know Trupp's foot hurt, just as she had known who he was. She hummed softly as she cleaned the cut on his paw. Then she covered it with a small bandage from a box she had pulled from a cart piled high with her belongings.

"Thank you, Bernice," said Trupp. "I'm Trupp."

"And I'm Krok," said the raven.

"What are you doing here?" Bernice asked. "This can be an extremely dangerous place after dark."

Lifting Trupp up into her cart, Bernice said to Krok, "C'mon, bird. It's time we got out of here. I'm going to take you two uptown where you'll be safer."

They rolled along the narrow, littered streets.

"Almost there," Bernice assured them. "I know several good places to eat and sleep."

Suddenly a man jumped at them from the shadows.

"It's Mad Moe," Bernice hissed. "He's terribly unpredictable."

With a toothless smile and amazing strength, Mad Moe charged the cart and roared, "Going uptown, eh? Well, I'll *uptown* you!"

Trupp, Krok, and everything Bernice owned went flying out onto the ground.

Terrified but not hurt, Trupp knew just what to do.

He pulled off his disguise and hopped in front of the man.

"Hey, you're a c-cat...or something like th-that," Mad Moe stammered.

Trembling, Trupp said, "Please leave us alone, or I may need to use my claws."

The man's toothless mouth gaped. He looked at Bernice and gasped, "You hear this thing talking?"

Bernice shrugged. "Don't hear a word."

The man clapped his hands over his ears and ran away, ducking as Krok swooped about his head.

Trupp dressed and everyone put the cart back in order. Soon they arrived uptown and sat down outside the back door of a restaurant.

"I love Italian food," Bernice said, "and the people who run this place like to share."

Passing a tray of garlic bread, Bernice pointed and said, "That's spaghetti on the side."

They all ate heartily—and with style.

Bellies full, they went to a park with green grass and lots of trees.

"My favorite spot," Bernice murmured as they lay drifting to sleep beneath an old, soft blanket. Then she chuckled. "Funny, isn't it? I wear all this bright stuff to keep from feeling invisible. When people stare at me, it helps me know I'm here. But Trupp puts on clothes so he will disappear."

Trupp sighed, "I'm glad *you* saw me. But I'm getting tired of wearing all these clothes. I want to go home."

"I know what you mean," Bernice said.

Early the next morning Bernice showed Trupp and
Krok to the edge of town.

"Thank you for not being afraid of me," said Trupp.
"Thank you for … everything."

Krok clucked in agreement.

Bernice smiled as she pinned the big yellow button
from her hat on Trupp's shirt. "Ah, but I should thank *you*.
It's not every day that I get the chance to help someone."

The illustrations in this book were done in
Liquitex acrylics and Prismacolor pencils on bristol board.
The display type was hand-lettered by Judythe Sieck.
The text type was set in Goudy Village.
Designed by Lisa Peters